TRAIN

CHARLES TEMPLE   *Illustrated by* **LARRY JOHNSON**

HOUGHTON MIFFLIN COMPANY
Boston 1996

To the great train poets,
Huddie Ledbetter and Jimmie Rodgers
C. T.

To my wife, Sharon, whose love, trust,
and support make the impossible possible
L. J.

For information about this and other Houghton Mifflin trade and reference
books and multimedia products, visit The Bookstore at Houghton Mifflin
on the World Wide Web at (http://www.hmco.com/trade/)

Manufactured in the United States of America

Typography by Ariel Apte
The text of this book is set in 14.5-point Corona Bold.
The illustrations are acrylic, reproduced in full color.

WOZ   10 9 8 7 6 5 4 3 2 1

LIBRARY OF CONGRESS CATALOGING-IN-PUBLICATION DATA
Temple, Charles A.
Train / by Charles Temple ; illustrated by Larry Johnson
p.   cm.   ISBN 0-395-69826-X
Summary: Everyone along the way enjoys the sight
and sound of the C & O train rolling down the rail.

[1. Railroads—Trains—Fiction.   2. Stories in rhyme.]
I. Johnson, Larry, ill.   II. Title.
PZ8.3.T2187Tr   1995   94-28256
[E]—dc20   CIP   AC

The train stands trembling on the C & O track,
As the whistle puffs a warning, loud and low.

Now the smoke comes chuffing from the short smokestack,
And the lights go sweeping,
And the engine goes rumbling,
And the wheels start squeaking kind of slow,

Past a wall—
'Cross a bridge—
By the circus and the junkyard and the jail.
And the wheels come squeaking,
And the smoke comes chuffing,
And the train comes rolling down the rail.

And a man—
In the jail—
Hears the sound and wonders where that train is gone,
As the whistle goes puffing,
And the engine goes rumbling,
And the train goes passing in the dawn.

When the sun shines high above the C & O track,
And the passengers are passing time away,
Some are dealing out a card game: king, queen, jack!

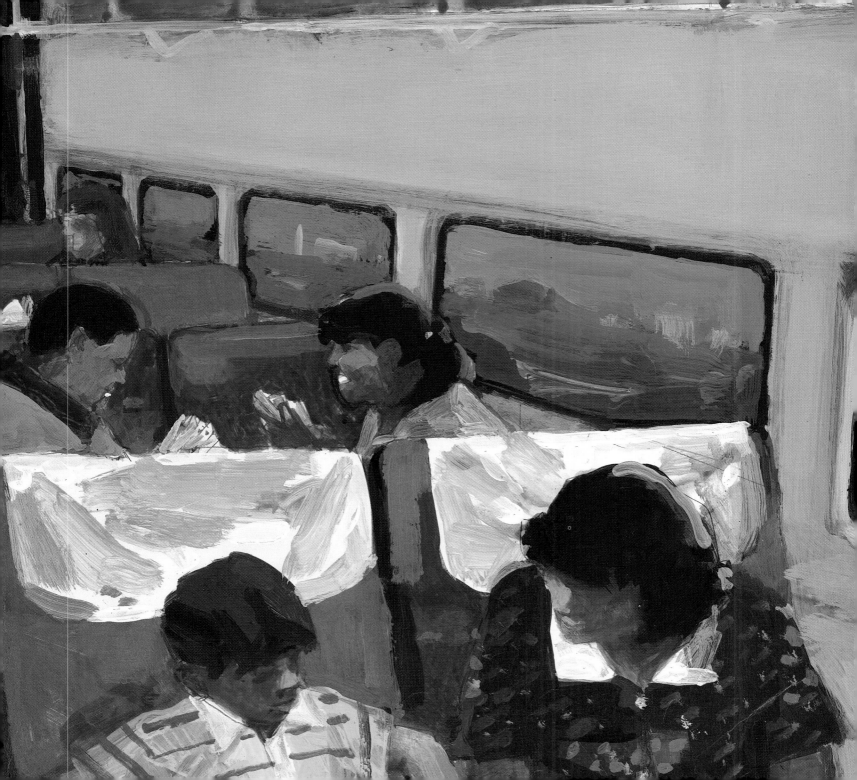

While the children come dancing,
And their beads come clicking,
And the mama comes shouting, "Now, hey!"

People chat—
People snooze—
People sit and watch the country pass along,
While the beads come clicking,
And the wheels come clacking,
And the whistle comes blowing low and strong.

And a girl—
In the corn—
Stops to listen as she leans upon her hoe.
And the whistle comes puffing,
And the wheels come clacking,
And the girl stands watching as they go.

When the sun goes setting on the C & O track,
And the dinner bell is ringing high and clear,
Dinner's waiting in the dining car, seven cars back.

Then the daddy comes ambling,
And the mama comes wobbling,
And the children come bounding toward the rear.
And the bumps—
And the curves—

Make the people stagger, stumble, lurch, and sway.
But the children keep bounding,
And the daddy keeps ambling,
And the mama keeps wobbling on her way.

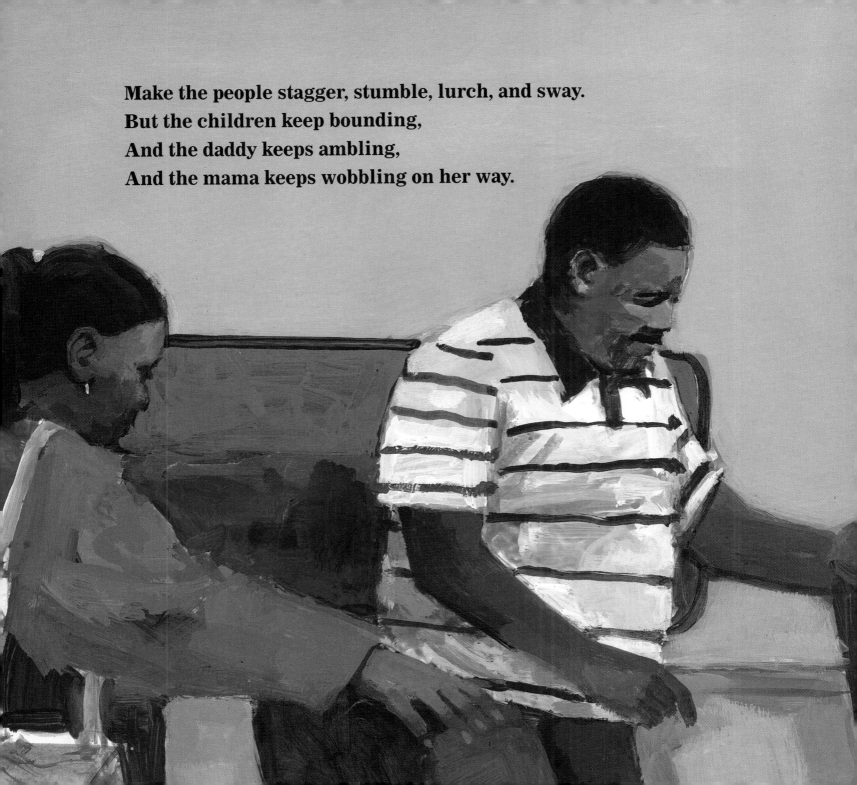

And the cows—
In the field—
Stop their grazing as they watch them rumble by.

And the folks keep swaying,
And the smoke keeps chuffing,
And the train goes passing on the fly.

When the stars come shining on the C & O track,
And the passengers are nodding heavy heads,
Then the people find the knob to make the seats lean back—
And the mama goes pushing,
And the children go laughing,
And the seats go turning into beds.

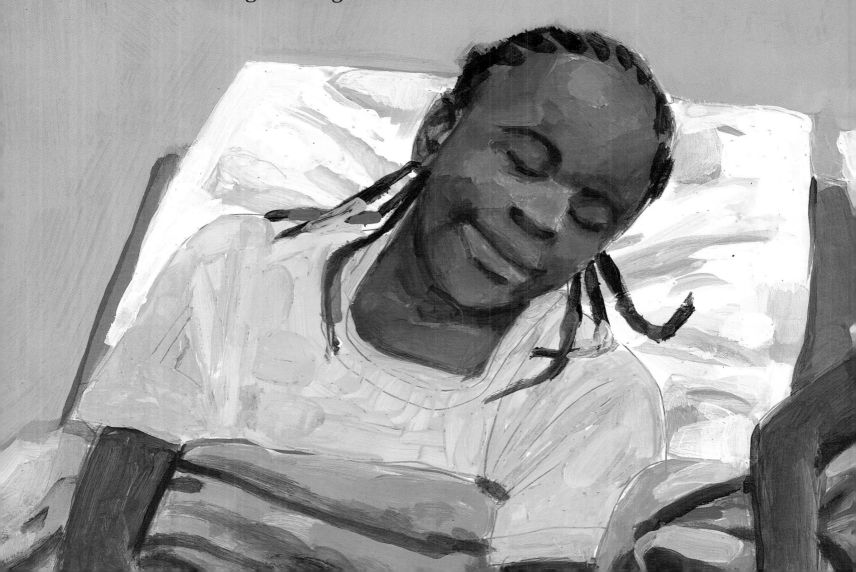

And the folks—
Snuggle down—
Cozy up and pull their blankets to their teeth.
And the cars keep rocking
And the engine keeps rumbling
And the wheels keep clacking underneath.

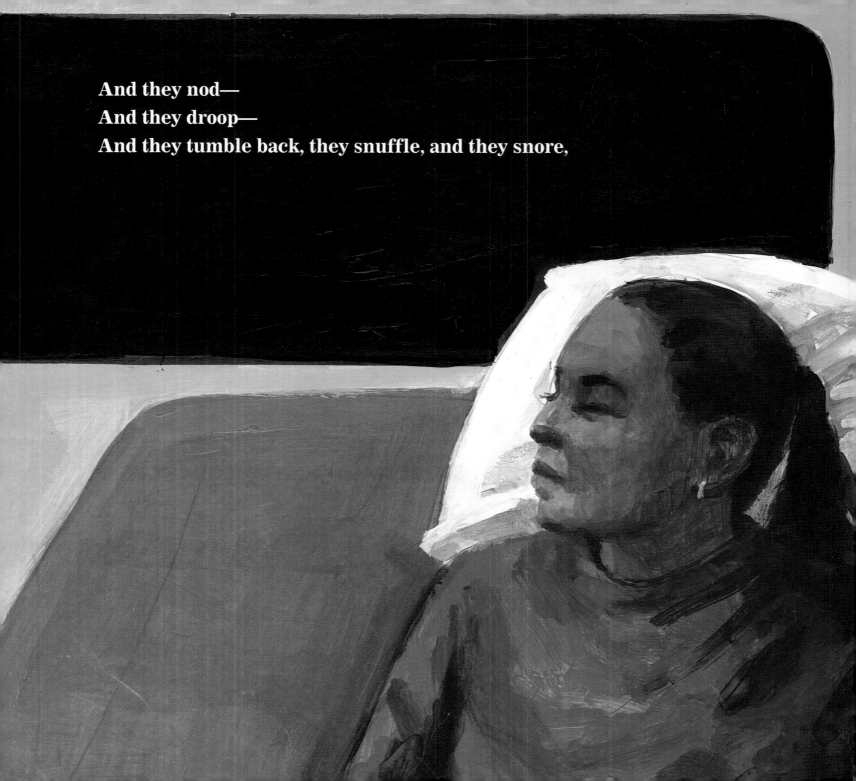

And they nod—
And they droop—
And they tumble back, they snuffle, and they snore,

While the smoke keeps chuffing,
And the train keeps rolling,
And the wheels keep clacking 'neath the floor.

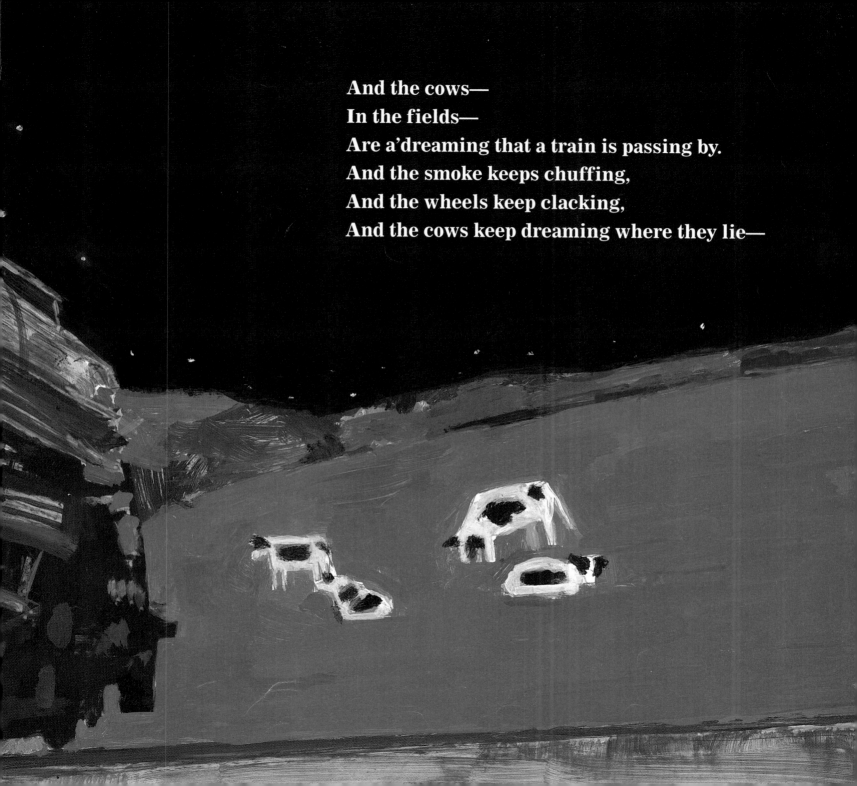

And the cows—
In the fields—
Are a'dreaming that a train is passing by.
And the smoke keeps chuffing,
And the wheels keep clacking,
And the cows keep dreaming where they lie—

And the smoke keeps chuffing,
And the wheels keep clacking,
And the cows keep dreaming where they lie.